Mike Warren

Warren

The

Cool

In

You

2

2

Mike Warren

Mike Warren Publishing

DEDICATION

This book is for us older

Brothas that still

Got it going on!!!

Mike Warren

Becool031@gmail.com

http://www.facebook.com/mike.warren.986

ACKNOWLEDGEMENTS

Wow, where do I begin? This past year has had many highs and many lows for me but through it all, I still made it through with no other help but my Lord and savior Jesus Christ. All praises to Him.

To my family who has been my biggest supporters thank you for your love, encouragement and patience.

To all of my fans that continue to support me in my work, I thank you and appreciate you, more than words can express.

To all the online talk shows, book clubs, book stores and online book clubs, thank you thank you thank you for giving my work a chance to hit mainstream media.

To the one and only model on the cover, Mr. Kent Barnes, I thank you for being so so sexy….especially for brothas in our age category and even for the younger ones, we both still got it going on!

To all my other writer friends, Dwayne Vernon, Ms. KTO aka Tammy, Mondell Pope, Shadrach Walker, Richardo Author Lore Harrison and all the rest, I thank you for your support and love.

And last but not least, to my Graphic Artist, Dominique Wilkens you are just absolutely fabulous!!!

Again, thank you all for your love and support!!!!

Mike Warren

Chapter 1

James L. Parker

I can't believe it's been almost a year since I took Nicolas aka Nicky into my home and to raise him as my own. It also hurt me to my heart when Nicky's father died. But at least I have a part of him in Nicky.

For those of you who don't know the story. I met Nicolas's father in the hospital when I had gone there to visit my nephew, Terrence aka Terry. Nicky's father was Terry's Doctor, Dr. Carroll Phillips.

To make a long story short, Carroll and I began dating and after a world wind romance, Carroll asked me to marry him and on the night he proposed, Carroll had a massive heart attack and died right there on the spot. What made matters worse was that Carroll had planned a huge party and invited family and friends to witness his proposal to me. After I said yes, Carroll was so happy that he apparently over exerted himself in dancing that he fell right on the floor and died.

I was mortified. I had been single for some time and all 3 of my children are grown and to be 52 years of age, I never thought I would meet someone and fall in love and start a new life, until Carroll came along.

Within a short period of time, I had buried my mother and had to attend my fiancés burial as well. I was so devastated I didn't know what I was going to do. As a bankruptcy attorney I have my own practice but I no longer cared about that or anything else.

After Carroll's funeral, his oldest daughter Rasheeda informed me that Carroll had left behind a 5 year old son, named, Nicolas. You see, Nicholas was being raised by Carroll's daughter and now that Carroll had died, she was no longer in a position to take care of him financially. She asked if I would take care of Nicky and raise him as my own. She hated to have to give him up but she felt as though her father would have wanted it that way. I jumped at the chance because I had no one else and I strongly believe that Nicky brought life back into my life.

The good news is, I submitted all of the paperwork a few months later and a couple of days ago; I received Nicky's adoption papers and he was now officially my son. Out of love for his deceased father, I made sure that Nicky kept his father's last name so that his heritage would continue on.

That being said today is a celebration of Nicky being a part of my family. I've invited my grown kids and their families, my friends, Angela, Juan, Ken, Frankie, my nephew, Terry, my secretary Sherry and the list goes on. There are going to be at least 50 people here at my home for the biggest cookout I have ever given.

"Pop-pop," Nicky said as he tried helping me prepare the food.

"Yeah son."

"So, this cookout is for me, right," he asked looking up at me.

"Yes, it is."

"Well, why don't we have a cake?"

"Why would you want a cake at a cookout," I asked looking at him strangely.

"I don't know. Why not, I like cake and so do many other people, so, why not?"

I really never gave it much thought until Nicky just inquired about it. I mean, who has cake at a cookout? However, as Nicky stated, most of us love cake, so why not? "Wow, Nicky you are something else. Well, I tell you what, why don't I have your big cousin Terry to stop at a bakery and bring a cake with him, how's that," I asked picking him up and sitting him down on the kitchen counter.

"That would be so cool," he smiled as he continued to watch me cook.

"Naw little man, what's cool is you," I replied while holding my hand out so he could slap it.

"You're cool too Pop-pop," he stated slapping my hand. And out of nowhere he asked, "Can we have a dog?"

"A dog?"

"Yeah, a big dog," he inquired.

"Why would you want a big dog?"

"Because my friend Zack from school has a big dog," he said as a matter of fact.

"Do you really think you're old enough to take on the responsibilities of a dog?"

"Yes," he smiled knowing that he wasn't.

"I can't even get you to keep your room clean, how you going to be able to take care of a dog, a big dog at that."

"Ok, well, can I get a cat?"

"Nicky."

"Yes."

"No."

"Well, can I get a fish?"

"What is with you today, asking about pets," I said laughing at him. I swear this little boy is a trip but I love him whole heartedly.

"I dunno, just making conversation," he answered looking dead at me.

"Conversation? Really." This boy cracks me up. There are times where he acts so grow up and there are other times where he's so vulnerable that I feel the need to protect him. It's funny, one minute he acts his age and the next he acts like he's 21 years old. However, he keeps me on my feet.

"So, how's work?"

"Work is work," I answered him while allowing him to rinse of the tomatoes under the water faucet. "How's summer camp? You'll be getting out soon and starting back to school. Are you excited?"

"Yeah, I guess."

"You are too much, you know that? But I love you just the same," I replied leaning over and kissing him on his forehead.

"Love you too Pop-pop."

"Ok then, well our guest will be arriving soon so why don't you go upstairs, clean up your room and change your clothes," I said while lifting him off the kitchen counter. "Dang son, you're getting too big."

"I'm not getting big Pop-pop, you just need to work out more," he said laughing while running up the stairs.

All I could do is shake my head. As my mother would say, 'That boy is sumf'n else!" When Nicky first came to my home, Nicky had noticed that on one of my living room walls, I have a "Wall of Fame" in essence pictures of my children from when they were younger and up until now. I noticed Nicky seemed to have felt left out because there were no pictures of him and I.

So, that he would feel more at home, I scheduled a photo shoot for the both of us. It was a little awkward mainly because the photographer was actually trying to hit on me while taking our picture. It's funny I still hadn't had that talk with Nicky about my lifestyle or the love that I shared with his father, other than to tell him that his father and I were very good friends. Nicky is now 6 years of age, how do you explain to a 6 year old that you love other men?

I was flattered that the photographer still found me to be attractive, but even though he wasn't a bad looking brotha, he had to only be in his late 20's or early 30's and God only knows, what could I do with that? Although, I'm sure the sex would be great but that's all it would be.

However, I did take advantage of the good deal the photographer had given me for the 20 frames of film we took. Both Nicky and I took photos with our Sunday best on as well as our every day clothing. And believe it or not, Nicky and I both loved the picture of our normal everyday clothing on standing back to back while I'm looking over my shoulder, down at him. I had the photographer to do a large 16x20 of that picture and it hangs all by itself on one of the side walls of my living room. I see Nicky looking at our picture every day with such pride on his face. I seriously do believe he now feels like he belongs, you know? Although, I know that I will have to have that talk about my lifestyle soon.

After I stopped day dreaming I began gathering some of the food and condiments to take out in the back yard and placed them on some of the tables. I looked around and everything was definitely in place the way I wanted things to be. Thank God Terry and Frankie came by early this morning and sat up the tables and umbrellas. I had about 10 or so of them and at least 10 people could sit at each one. I pulled out my cell phone to give Terry a call. He answered on the first ring.

"Waddup Unc," Terry said so cheerfully answering his phone.

"Where are you? Are you on your way over?"

"I was about to leave in a few, why?"

"Well, could you stop at a bakery or something and bring a cake?"

"A cake? Unc, this is a cookout not a birthday party. Geeesh, you getting old Unc," Terry laughed into the phone.

"Terry I know it's not a birthday party but Nicky wants a cake. So, if you don't mind, would you pick up one, please?"

"Ok Unc, ok, just messing witcha. How's little Nicky anyway?"

"He's cool," I laughed. "He's upstairs getting dress. I bought him a new outfit yesterday and he wants to show it off for everyone."

"Will you stop."

"Stop, stop what?"

"Ah, nuf'n Unc. Anyway, I'll pick up a cake and bring it with me, a'ight?"

"Ok, see you soon."

I hung up the phone and I don't know what's going on with Terry but for the past year he has been acting very strange. Not to mention that he and Frankie have been getting along better than before. I remember when they couldn't stand one another and now, it's like they're the best of friends. Something is definitely going on with him. I guess I'll wait until Monday I'll talk with him at work. For now, I just want to enjoy this day without any drama with Nicky, family and friends.

Terrence aka Terry

"See, why is it when I'm on the phone with my Unc, you gotta act a fool."

"Because we love each other and you won't tell James or anybody that you and I are lovers. That's why," Frankie said climbing on my lap and planting kisses all over my face.

Frankie is right I have yet to tell anybody about us mainly because I'm not sure if I'm ready to come out as they say. I mean, I'm still in my 20's and have been a womanizer ever since the age of 15. I've always been attracted to older sophisticated women; you know those who are considered sugar mommas?

It's funny, at the beginning I didn't like Frankie at all and the feeling was mutual. However, one particular night while in a drunken somber, Frankie took advantage of me. I don't recall what really happened but he tells me that I loved every minute of it. Personally, I find that hard to believe. I've been loving pussy far too long for that to be true.

That being said, once again I found myself in a drunken state but not so drunk that I didn't know what was going on. This time around, I seduced Frankie. I was curious and since that night we've been together ever since. Shawty had it going on in the sex department.

Unfortunately, and as much as I have love for Frankie, I constantly have to hear his mouth about me being Angela's baby daddy. A while back, Angela and I hooked up and we were cool. She was one of my sugar mommas but something happened, she changed. She started treating me like I was her property instead of treating me like her man. So, even though we have gone each other's way, we still co-parent my beautiful daughter Brittany who is only a couple of months old today. I have no regrets in my relationship with Angela, even though she was old enough to be my momma but she gave me a child and I love my daughter with all my heart.

Now, if I can only get Frankie off my back and stop him from criticizing everything I do. I mean he talks about how I dress, he constantly wanting me to pull my pants up, he criticize the music I listen to, he talks about me spending more time with my daughter, he criticize me all the time. The one thing he doesn't criticize about is how I fuck him. I guess that's a good thing. Again, I do love him, I just don't know why?

Chapter 2

Juan Johnson

"Are you dress or not," I asked Ken on the phone because we were going to James's cookout together. He claimed he didn't feel like driving.

"Dang, why you so angry, I'm getting dress now."

"Well, you know James will have a fit if we're not there on time. You know how he is," I hissed into the phone.

"Personally, I don't think anything could put James in a bad mood today. You heard how happy he was when he told us that he was approved for Nicky's adoption."

"This is true but you were suppose to be ready an hour ago."

"Well, if you get off the phone and let me finish dressing I would have been," he spat.

"Ready or not, I'll be there in 15 minutes and you better be outside waiting."

I hung up the phone because I knew that if I didn't Ken would have continued talking for the next hour or so. We still seem to go at one another on occasions but we are the best of friends and have known each other for years. So, I'm glad that we were able to move on with our love and friendship for one another.

What really put a strain on our friendship was of course a man. Last year, we found out that we were dating the same man and neither one of us wanted to let him go. Fortunately, we realized that our friendship was more important that any man. So, being the bigger person, I stopped seeing this man and Ken and I have been closer than ever. He still gets on my nerves but that another story.

§§§§§§

Kenneth Hutchins aka Ken

Juan sometime thinks he's everyone's mother and tries to tell people what to do. But I'm not the one. My mother pass away some time ago and can I help it that it takes longer for me to get it together then the rest?

Not much have changed with me this pass year. I'm still single and looking to mingle, if you know what I mean? Well, if I'm going to be really honest, my health seems to have gotten worse. I don't want to tell the gang because the last thing I need them to do is worry about me. Other than the pain that I get from time to time in my back, my HIV status has begun to show in my appearance. A year ago my blood work count was so on point that I was considered undetectable.

However, as of last week, my white blood cell count has been low and I've been losing a pound here and there. At 53, I still want to live a long life and enjoy being around my family and friends. I realize at some point that I will have to let the gang know about what's really going on with me but until then, maybe we can just enjoy James and little Nicky's union as father and son.

What really shocked me this past year is my girl Angela. You know Ms. Thing had the nerve to give birth to a baby girl? Ms. Thing is 53 like me and there is no way I could see raising a newborn let alone give birth to one. The funny thing is Terry is Angela's baby daddy. Chile, I screamed for days when I found out. But, I do wish Angela the very best because I do have love for her, she is my girl.

§§§§§

Angela Dobson aka Angela

I must have been out of my mind thinking I could have a newborn baby at my age. Don't get me wrong, I love my baby girl, I really do but within these last 2 months, I think I've cried more than she has. And as for her daddy, Mr. Terrence "Womanizer" Parker, he ain't shit.

As soon as I told him he was going to be a daddy, he hauled ass. Talking about I'm not the father. That pissed me off because first of all, I'm not a hoe. Secondly, I wasn't with anyone else during that time. Hell, I'm 53 years old I know who the father of my baby is.

Nonetheless, I've been changing diapers back to back last night, early morning feedings, giving baths and rocking her sleep. By the time I done all of that, I'm tired my damn self. Personally, I think I'm suffering from post pardon depression, PPD. Seems like every time my baby cry, I cry and I know that's not a good thing. I'm crying because she's crying and when I pick her up and she looks at me, I feel like she's crying because I'm crying. Something definitely got to give.

I took a one year sabbatical and fortunately, I will be returning to work in another month or so. To be honest, I've missed being a criminal defense attorney. The excitement I would get when walking into a court room and all eyes on me while I defend some of the worse criminals in Charlotte, North Carolina; the joy of getting a jury to smile and nod in agreement as I give my opening statements. Negotiating with other attorney's and the wit of words with one another is who and what I am. Being a mother of a newborn may not be the best thing for me at this time.

However, I will laugh and smile while attending James' cookout and the celebration of welcoming Nicky into his family. Deep down, I am happy for James, especially after losing a mother and a lover all in one year. James deserves happiness and I pray nothing but the best for the both of them.

§§§§§

James Jr.

"So, you think this is a good thing for dad," I asked my younger sister, Michelle on the phone.

"I don't see why not. I mean besides, we're grown now and dad has nothing else to do but work and come home to an empty house. He needs the sound of pitter patter around the house," she laughed into the phone.

"So, you all for the idea I see. What about Valerie, have you spoken to her?"

"Actually I talked with her last night. Her flight should be coming in an hour. I'm on my way out to the airport now to pick her up."

"So, she's all for this as well, huh," I asked sucking my teeth.

"Junior, what's going on with you? Don't you want dad to be happy?"

"Sure, I want him to be happy but I don't think adopting a child and splitting our inheritance in 4 ways is something I'm down with. Now, I know that might sound kind of selfish but that's how I feel," I hissed.

"Junior, really, so this is about the money for you?"

"And what's wrong with that? I know I can't be the only one that feels this way."

"Well, I don't have an issue with it and I don't think Valerie has an issue with it. Where are you anyway?"

"I'm driving down on Rte 77, I should be at dad's house within the next hour, why?"

"Did you bring my nieces and nephews?"

"Naw, not this time," I sighed.

"And why not? You know how daddy is he wants the whole family present. He made that very clear. So why didn't you bring them?"

"To be honest, I don't see this as a celebration so why am I gonna bring my whole family up from Philly just to come all the way down here for?"

"Because dad wanted it."

"Well, dad must be going through menopause or a midlife crisis and I think that we should all get together and talk with him to make sure he's doing the right thing."

"Well, you gonna talk to him by yourself.

You know when dad has his mind made up, there's nothing anyone can do."

"We'll see about that," I spat.

"Boy, you're a trip. Well, look, I'll see you at dad's I'm about to find a parking spot here at the airport."

"Oh ok, I'll see you when you get there."

Once I hung up from my sister, I couldn't believe that she and my other sister all seem to be good with this adoption thing for my dad. I'm sorry, but as the oldest, I refuse to stand by and watch my dad do something he's going to regret later. Especially, if it has anything to do with my inheritance; the boy might need a father figure, the boy might even need my dad to raise him but the boy is not blood and therefore should not be entitled to anything that my father might leave behind after his demise.

I know this might make me sound like an ass but as one of Philadelphia's finest, I see families go through this all the time. There is always a battle over money when someone dies and the last thing I need is to let that happen in my own family.

Chapter 3

James

Three hours in and my cookout was in full swing. Everyone who was invited came including my ex-wife and her husband, the good Reverent.

I had Terry over at the grille with all the meats, hamburgers, hotdogs, chicken, etc…and I had Frankie over at the bar serving anything and everything depending on what people wanted.

Both Juan and Ken was helping me co-host the event by making sure people had everything they needed. My girl Angela just looked like she hadn't slept in days.

"Angela, are you ok, sweetie," I asked walking up to her at the bar.

"James, I think Ms. Thang here is wore out from motherhood," Frankie laughed.

"I'm fine if you must know. Anyway, can I have my Martini please," she said to Frankie with a hint of sarcasm.

"Coming right up," Frankie replied.

"So, how's my niece," I asked.

"She's fine, my neighbors daughter Joanne is babysitting. So, how's my little nephew?"

"Which one," I asked laughing.

"You know damn well who I'm talking about, Master Nicky," she laughed.

"Here's your Martini," Frankie said interrupting our conversation.

"Thank you, paid help is so hard to fine, isn't it," Angela said as she walked away from the bar.

"What's her problem," Frankie asked me.

"I don't know, I guess motherhood is getting the best of her," I shrugged.

"Well, Ms. Thang needs to go and talk to someone if you know what I mean."

"By that you mean a shrink?"

"Shrink, therapist or some dayum body cause she keep on with that mouth of hers, she will get read. I'm just saying."

"Ok Frankie, I'll talk to her some other time. However, I have over a hundred guest and we are here to celebrate. No drama, you understand," I said pointing my finger at Frankie.

Angela

"So, when are you going to pay child support for your daughter," I asked walking over to Terry as he burns the meat up on the grille.

"Child support, really Angela, you come here just to ask me for me child support? Is that how you doing it now," he asked angrily.

"Well, I'm just saying. She's 2 months old and you have brought her an outfit or two as well as some diapers. Is that all you think it takes to raise a baby?"

"No, Angela I don't however, do you mind if we talk about this some other time?"

"Oh my, you sound so angry," I stated as I walked away with a smile on my face.

Ken

"James, I think this is a fabulous cookout darling," I said walking up to him and kissing him on the cheek.

"Well, I'm glad you approve," he smiled kissing me back.

"So, where's the little prince, Nicky? Don't tell me you've misplaced the child already," I laughed.

"No, he went upstairs to prepare."

"Prepare, prepare for what," I asked looking at James strangely.

"It's a surprise," he said smiling and walking away.

"Oh no he didn't," I said to myself.

James Jr.

"Like I said, I don't think this is a good idea. Besides, don't y'all think dad is too old to be raising a 6 year old boy," I asked Valerie and Michelle as we stood around in the kitchen having our pow-wow.

"Junior, as long as daddy is happy, we should be happy. I don't see why you just don't let it go," my youngest sister Michelle stated.

"Valerie, how do you feel about all this," I asked looking in her direction.

"Personally, I'm with Michelle on this one Jr. I mean, daddy is what, 52 now? Let him enjoy whatever it is he wants to do with his life. You really just need to get over it. Besides, I like having Nicky as a little brother, he's so cool."

"That little boy just got y'all fooled. He

knows what he's doing," I answered while drinking the rest of my beer.

"Junior, he's 6 years old, what is he doing," Michelle asked as she and Valerie laughed at me.

"Whatever, I replied as I walked out of the kitchen.

"Hey James Junior," Angela said as she walked up to me.

"Ah, Angela, right," I asked not knowing for sure.

"Yes, the name is Angela. You must have a short term memory or would that be considered long term memory," she laughed.

"What are you talking about," I asked looking at her strangely.

"Humph, never mind," she stated as she sucked her teeth and walked away.

"Bitch," I mumbled under my breath.

Juan

"Excuse me, can I have you guys attention. Hello, Hello…Can I have you guys attention?" Once people stopped talking and I had everyone's attention, I began, "Can I have everyone in the living room please. The host, our friend, James have asked me to have you guys come into the living room for a minute. Can we do that?"

People eventually began to gather in the living room. I checked out into the backyard to make sure everyone had gotten the message and they apparently did because no one was out there. I walked into the living room and stood in the middle of the room, "First of all, I'd like to thank each and every one of you guys for coming out and celebrating the new addition to the Parker family. I know for the past hour or so, people have asked me where's James and Nicky? Well, they have asked me to get you guys all together so that they can do a performance for you guys, just to say thank you all. Ok, Frankie, play the sound track."

The soundtrack of Baby face's old jam, "For The Cool In You," had started up and much to every one's surprise, both James and Nicky came down the staircase, taking one step at a time in rhythm of the song wearing matching Zoot Suits. Nicky's was a bright yellow color and James was a bright royal blue as well as they both wore wide brim Derby's. Everyone fell out, James and Nicky looked so cool in their suits and just watching them mouthed the words to Baby face's song brought back memories of watching the old "Cosby Show" when the Huxtables use to do the same thing for their family.

They were so good, family and friends starting throwing out money in the center of the floor. People pulled out their phones and began videotaping it as well. "Y'all betta werk," Frankie yelled, while getting closing with his cell phone in hand.

Watching both Nicky and James slide across the floor from one side all the way over to the other side while they lip sang was awesome. Hell, I didn't even know James could dance like that.

"Nicky is just too cute and can dance, look at him," Ken said pulling on his fake pearls.

"He sure can," others said in agreement.

"Do it baby," Angela yelled smiling from ear to ear.

Just as the song was coming to an end, Nicky began climbing the staircase, just as he made it to the top; he did a Michael Jackson move and people roared in laughter and applause. Then it was James time to climb the steps and do the same as Nicky but by the time James made it to the top, he was so tired, all he could do is fall out, and not to be out done, but Nicky fell out on top of James.

Everyone kept laughing and applauding because the performance that James and Little

Nicky gave, we all yelled, "Encore, encore, encore."

James

"Hold on, let me catch my breath," I said to Nicky as he tried helping me up from the floor.

"See, you did it. You're not that old. Although, I was better than you," Nicky said laughing at his own joke.

I finally got up from the floor and as I began walking down the staircase, people continued to shout and applaud our performance. As soon as Nicky and I got to the center of the floor, I took a deep breath and said, "Lawd, give me strength." People looked at one another and began to laugh. "I'm serious, trust and believe when I tell you, this was not my idea. This was Nicky's idea so all the applause should go to him." I then turned to Nicky and said, "You wanna say something little man?"

"Naw, you go ahead," he replied acting bashful while wrapping his arms around my leg.

"Anyway, we both wanted to do something special just to say thank you for all the support you guys have given us within the past year. We appreciate all of you and I also want to introduce Rasheeda Phillips to you guys. For those of you who don't know who Rasheeda is, she is Nicky's oldest sister." Rahseeda came up and stood beside me and Nicky. "I personally wanted to take this time out and thank you for bringing Nicky into my life because if it had not been for him, I don't know where I would be right now. So, thank you, I love you and you are also a part of this family," I said as I hugged and kissed both Rasheeda and Nicky.

James Jr.

"Oh I see, dad just lost his damn mind now," I replied leaning over and whispered in my sister, Michelle's ear.

"What are you talking about? You didn't like the little dance they just did? I thought it was fabulous," she said looking at me like I'm crazy.

"I'm not talking about that. I'm talking about dad now inviting this ghetto whatever into our family. I guess she's gonna share in the inheritance as well, huh?

Chapter 4

James

Fortunately, the cookout was a huge success everyone seemed to have had a ball of a time. Even as I began escorting some of the guest out to their cars, I received invites for me and Nicky to do that again at their various events. As flattered as I was, I knew that wasn't going to happen again. They might have thought I was joking and playing around but that really took a lot out of me. Hell, I'm not as young as I used to be but I had to admit, I was looking pretty damn good in this Zoot Suit.

Minutes later, all of my kids, including Nicky chipped in and helped me clean up the mess that every one made. I will admit, I love throwing a party but it's the clean up part I hate. But then suddenly, I began to hear someone yelling outside and it sound like Angela. I went to my front door and sure enough, standing on my driving pad was Angela and Terry arguing about child support and he was a no good father.

"Angela, really, you going to do this now," I asked getting in between her and Terry.

"James, this has nothing to do with you. Terrence knows what he suppose to be doing and he ain't doing it," she hissed.

"Look, I told you I was doing the best I can. I don't make the kinda money you make so I can't do as much but at least I'm trying," Terry said getting angry.

"Angela, can you come in the house for a minute so I can talk to you? As for you Terry, I will talk to you later, just leave, now!"

I escorted Angela in my house and we decided to go back out in the backyard. "Would you like something to drink," I offered.

"Yes, if you don't mind," she replied with a little attitude.

I went to the bar, poured two glasses of Zinfandel and handed her a glass as I took a seat next to her.

"Now Angela, what's going on with you?"

"What do you mean what's going on with me," she spat.

"Angela, you are one of the best criminal

attorney's here in Charlotte but yet not two minutes ago, you're yelling out on my parking pad at yo baby daddy. This is not like you. You knew going into this that Terry didn't make a lot of money and he sure wasn't the kind of man that you would want to have a baby by. So, again I ask, what's going on with you?"

While waiting for a response, Angela just broke down and started crying. I really felt bad for her because I know it can't be easy on her and I know she feels that she's becoming one of those kinds of women that she despises so. I placed my arms around her to let her know that I still cared and loved her very much.

"James, I…I…I don't kn..know what I'm go…going to do," she said through tears.

"What's wrong," I asked being concern.

"I'm…I'm too old James to be raising a baby. I just can't do it," she confessed.

"Yes you can, it just takes patience

besides, you've done it 3 times before," I replied trying to make her feel better.

"James, I was almost 30 years younger too," she laughed through tears.

"I know, we both were."

"See, with Nicky, it's not too bad, he can kind of take care of himself. With a newborn, it's waking up at all hours of the night, changing diapers, feeding and that ship has already sailed for me. That's just not who I am anymore. I don't know what happen to my maternal instincts but they are not there anymore," she said while laying her head on my shoulder.

"So, Angela, what are you saying," I asked holding her chin up while looking her in the eye.

"What I'm saying James is that Terry is the father and I think he should be the one to raise her. Hell, I'll pay him child support," she stated in a serious tone.

"Wow, Angela, I just can't see Terry taking on that kind of responsibility. I mean, I don't even know what he's been doing with his life these past few months."

"He has a job, he still works for you, correct," she asked looking up at me sniffling.

"Yeah, he does but as you know, Terry is more of a womanizer. I can't see him taking on being a father full time."

"I'll take him to court and then he won't have a choice."

"Take him to court for what, Angela," I asked becoming upset.

"Look, I know that's your nephew and everything but I'll make sure that Terry at least get joint custody because right now I'm doing it all and that's just not fair to me."

"Well, Angela, I can't stop you from doing what you have to do and if it were anyone else other then my nephew I would be telling you to do what you gotta do. So, I'm going to tell you, do what you got to do.

§§§§§

Frankie

"You know she is really starting to get on my last nerve. I know that's yo baby momma but Terry, I can't just sit back and watch her yell at you the way she does without me wanting to cuss her ass out. But, I can't do that because for the past year, we have been keeping our relationship a fucking secret and I'm getting really tired," I said to Terry as we drove home.

"I know Bae, but now is not a good time for me to come out of the closet or whatever you wanna call it, you feel me?"

"No, Terry, I don't feel you. It's been almost a year, you need to shit or get off the pot as my momma used to say."

"I know Bae, I know, you're right. But how?"

"Look, I'm not saying you ought to have a parade or a party announcing your love for me but we can at least tell James and then maybe he could help in some way."

"I do like his parties doe," he began to laugh.

"Hahaha, very funny. I'm serious and you should be as well."

"I know Bae, you're right," he replied while leaning over and trying to kiss me on the cheek.

"Whoa, don't even try it," I said pulling away from him.

"Oooo weee, I like it we you get angry at me. You gonna let me hit that when we get home, right," he asked giving me his sexy smile and trying to feel on my backside.

"See, you think everything can be solved by having sex and it can't."

"I know Bae, but I really need you man. I mean, there's just a lot of bullshit going on right now and I know I have to step up and be a man and take care of it but for now, can't I get some love, some encouragement," he said pouting at me.

"Boy, you are so lucky that I love yo ass," I answered smiling at him.

§§§§§

Ken

"So, what did you think of James and Nicky's dance routine," I asked Juan as he drove me home.

"I thought it was cute and those suits were fabulous. I wonder if he bought those or whether he had them made?"

"Knowing James, he probably had them made."

"Oh, and did you hear Angela and Terry go at it as we were leaving?"

"Sho did, I think the whole block heard them," I replied laughing.

"You know, I really can't blame terry on this one. I mean, Angela had no business getting into a sexual relationship with Terry to begin with. I'm just saying."

"Hey, Juan."

"Yeah," I said keeping my eyes on the road.

"Can I tell you something?"

"Sure."

"You promise not to say anything."

"Of course I wouldn't. You're my best friend, why would I?"

"Ah, ah,…" I stopped myself because I was going to tell Juan about my health condition but I think I should wait until I see my doctor on Monday. Hopefully, he might have some good news for me.

"Ah, hello…you were saying," Juan asked interrupting my thoughts.

"Oh, it's nothing. Don't worry about it."

"Are you sure, I mean we can talk about anything right?"

"Of course, we can always talk, I just can't bring a man around yo stealing ass," I laughed trying to change the subject.

"Oh no you didn't."

"Oh yes I did."

"Get yo ass out of my car," I said as I pulled up to his house.

"Bitch please, you ain't said nothing but a word," he laughed as he got out of my car.

"Love you man."

"Love you more."

Chapter 5

James

"Good morning Mr. Parker," Sherry greeted me as I walked into my office.

"Good morning. Do you have any coffee ready because I could surely use a cup," I asked as I sat my briefcase on my desk and sat in my chair.

"I just made some, coming right up."

"Are these all the cases that need to be filed here on my desk," I yelled to Sherry out in the outer office.

"Yes, I just put them there just before you came in."

"Oh ok cool, is Terry here yet," I asked picking up the files and going through them.

"No not yet. Here's your coffee. And for the record, I think you need to keep yo day job," she giggled.

"What do you mean, you didn't like my performance at the cookout?"

"Like I said, keep yo day job," again she giggle. "But, I did have a good time, thanks for inviting me."

"Your welcome, I saw you were all booed up, who was the lucky fellow?"

"His name is Sherman, oooo, I hate that name. I was going to introduce you to him but you were kinda busy at the cookout, so."

"Sherman, Sherman, Sherman," I said clapping my hands and bouncing up and down in my seat.

"That's not even funny," she replied going back into the outer office.

"I swear, you have no sense of humous," I laughed.

"Hey Unc, what's shaking," Terry asked smiling from ear to ear, walking in my office and taking a seat across from me.

"I don't know, you tell me," I asked looking at him.

"Nothing just chillin. How many cases we

need to file this morning," he asked trying to change the subject.

"Can you close my door, please?"

"Not a problem Unc," he replied getting up and closing my door.

"So, what are you going to do about Angela?"

"Dayum Unc, I don't know. She's just acting like a Bitch about the situation, you know," he stated as he crossed his legs.

"Well, can you blame her?"

"Dayum Unc, you sound like you're on her side," he scoffed.

"I'm not on anybody side but you have to understand that Angela is having a hard time raising your daughter by herself."

"Look Unc, I try to do what I can when it comes to clothes, diapers, formula…"

"See Terry, it's not even about the money. Angela has more than enough money to take care of your daughter. She just needs you to give her a break sometimes and get your daughter and keep her for a weekend or a week."

"Unc, what am I going to do with an infant for a whole weekend?"

"You should have thought about that before you started dicking her. I'm just tryna keep it real like you young people say."

"Unc, seriously, I don't see that happening," he replied leaning back in his chair.

"Well, I tell you what, you can either step up to the plate and do it on your own or have Angela take you to court and have a judge make you, you decide?"

"So, that's what she told you? She wants to take me to court?"

"Ah, yeah!"

"See, dat bit…"

"Whoa, hold up nephew." I said cutting him off. "You both are at fault and you have no reason to start calling her out of her name. Y'all wanted this so as my grandfather used to say, "You make your bed hard, now you have to lie down in it.""

"Unc, really," he began to laugh.

"What, it's true," I answered while trying not to laugh.

"See, you old people always gotta have a saying," he continued to laugh.

"Anyway, you need to set up a time where you and Angela can talk and so that you can give her a break. I don't know what you have been doing lately and I don't know who you been spending your time with but you are a father now and you need to put your personal life on hold for a minute and bond with your child. Now, I've done said what I have to say. So, let's do some work, is that cool with you?"

"Cool, Unc."

§§§§§

James Jr.

"Well, looka here, I thought y'all left last night," I said walking into my father's kitchen and seeing my sister's making morning breakfast. "Hmmm, smells good. Let me find out y'all can cook," I replied while pouring myself a cup of coffee.

"Listen who's talking, don't you have a family to go back to in Philly," Valerie hissed. "And how are my nieces and nephews, big head," she stated popping me upside my head while sitting across from me.

"They're fine and watch that," I replied while rubbing my head.

"So, are you feeling any better about the adoption or are you still pissed about it," my youngest sister Michelle asked.

"Why should my opinion change?"

"Well, I figured after this weekend…"

"Why, just because dad and this boy got together and did a little song and dance, we all suppose to forget everything and act like everything is alright," I asked cutting her off.

"So, you still hadn't talk with dad about how you feel," Michelle asked.

"No, not yet, but I plan to tonight and I

was hoping that you guys would be there for support."

"Just so you know, I don't have a problem in being there for having this family discussion but for the record, I think what daddy is doing is a wonderful thing and if it makes him happy, then I'm all for it," Michelle stated.

"Me too," Valerie agreed.

"Well dayum, can't a brotha at least get some breakfast?"

§§§§§

Ken

You know every time I come and see my doctor I'm always so on edge. I don't know whether he's going to give me good news or bad news. And being in the moving and hauling profession for so many years, I've got what they call, "*Spondylolisthesis.*" Which is

a spinal condition that involves the slipping of
one spinal vertebra over the one immediately
underneath it. So, as a result, I'm in pain 75%
of the time. The good news is that I've been
given pain killers called, *"Lorazepam"* to be
honest it's really not a pain killer but it helps
relax my muscles and therefore takes away
the pain.

The problem seems to be with the
medications I'm taking for my HIV status
along with other medicines that one takes
while getting older, they all don't seem to get
along with one another.

And to be honest, I'm scared to death of
dying. I think the fear lies in not knowing
what's on the other side. I mean, people will
always say, "Well, at least there's no more
pain," how do they know that? I think if you
believe in Heaven and hell, we're going to go
to one or the other and if your last destination
is in hell, well, guess what? The real pain just
got started.

And why is it when you have a doctor's appointment for a particular time, you really don't see the doctor until 30 or 45 minutes later? I guess that's the real reason why we are called patients. Hell, we have to be patient because by the time you do get to see your doctor, your blood pressure has already skyrocketed and then they look at you and wonder why your pressure is so high. I remember dating this one guy who worked in a doctor's office and he told me that doctor's will always overbook just to make sure that even if there is a cancellation, they still have a full caseload of patience's. *Sonsofbitches.*

"Mr. Hutchins, the doctor will see you now," the old white nurse said as she walked out into the waiting room.

I got up and followed her into the back offices. She escorted me into one of the rooms and began taking my vitals. "So, how are we feeling today," she asked making small talk.

Another ritual I hate about going to the doctor's office. The staff always wants to know how you're doing. One day I'm going to be honest and tell them *sonsofbitches* how pissed I am for having to wait all damn day. But until then, I replied, "Ah, fair to midland."

"I see your pressure is kind of high, 175/90," she stated as she took the band off from around my arm.

I wanted to tell her to kiss my ass and go and get the damn doctor but instead I just replied, "That's just how it do. One day its high and the next day it's low. Whatcha gonna do?"

"Ok then, the doctor will be in shortly," she stated as she left the room.

You know, for the amount of money they get paid, you would think they would at least have TV's in the rooms so patience can finish watching the Maury Show, which was showing out in the waiting area, I thought to myself. Now, I don't know who the dayum baby daddy is!

"Ah, good morning Mr. Hutchins, how are you feeling today," my doctor asked as he walked into the room.

"Like I told the nurse fair to midland, but again, you're the doctor so you tell me," I sighed.

"Well Mr. Hutchins, unfortunately, it's not good," he answered while sitting down and pulling his chair up closer to me.

"Why, what you mean," I asked becoming scared.

"The test that we got back from when you were here the last time shows things appear to have gotten worse," he said in a soft tone.

"Ok, so what are you saying," I asked bracing myself for the worse.

"Well, Ken, I'm gonna give it to you straight, unless we change your medication around and do it quickly, you're not going to survive," he said placing his hand on my shoulder.

"So, what are you saying, I'm gonna die," I asked still not believing what he was trying to say.

"Look, I've arranged for an ambulance to take you directly over to Carolinas Medical Center off of Blythe Blvd. Is there anyone you would like us to call?"

Just then, my life seemed to have flashed before my eyes. I was looking at death's door and didn't even know it. The sad thing is, I didn't have a partner or lover for them to even contact. I had my friends, James, Juan, Angela and even Frankie but, I didn't have a true love of my own.

"No, I don't have anyone you can call," I replied with water in my eyes as I looked down at the floor in total despair of my being.

Chapter 6

James

Monday's are such a crazy day being a bankruptcy attorney not to mention a very long day. However, being able to now come home to someone who needs me makes it all worthwhile. It gives a person's life purpose to just get up each day and do what you have to do. When you're young, you really don't think about getting old and having no one in your life to either grow old with and/or having someone in your life that needs and depend on you. Nicky does this for me.

"Good evening, I'm home," I said raising my voice as I entered my home. "Where is everyone," I asked walking from the living room and all the way out to the kitchen.

"Hey dad, we're out here," my daughter Valerie yelled.

"Well, I see you guys are enjoying the leftovers from the cookout along with the drinks," I stated as I walked out into my backyard.

"Hey daddy, how was your day? Would you like something to drink," my youngest daughter, Michelle asked.

"Hmmm, yeah, I guess I could have a cold glass of Chardonnay," I replied sitting down on one of my lawn chairs.

"So dad, can I ask you something," James Jr. asked.

"Oh Lawd," Valerie mumbled.

"Sure son, what's going on?"

"Well, the girls and I were wondering..."

"Whoa, don't even try it. You mean you because Valerie and I weren't wondering anything, ok," Michelle said handing me my glass of wine and rolling her neck from side to side at Junior.

"Ok, ok, I was wondering about Nicky," James Jr. stated.

"What about Nicky?"

"Well, I was wondering about this whole adoption thing."

"And," I asked.

"I mean, is this just temporary until such time his family can come for him?"

"No Jr. this is not temporary and at this point we are his family. So, what are you trying to say?"

"What he tryna say dad is, will Nicky gonna be in your will," Valarie scoffed.

"So, is this what this is about? You

worried about what you going to get when I'm no longer here," I asked looking over at my son with disappointment in my eyes.

"Look dad, I'm not trying to make it sound all that bad. I'm just saying that I'm the oldest of your children and I feel the need to speak up because the bottom line is, we're your blood, he's not," Jr. stated in an agitated tone.

"Well, I'm sorry you feel that way, I really am. So, let's just get to the chase, how much inheritance you think you're going to get once I'm dead and gone," I asked looking him dead in the eyes.

"What you mean," he asked looking at me strangely.

"I wanna know, how much do you think you're going to get upon my demise?"

"I'm don't know, I mean with the house, furniture, stocks, life insurance policies, I guess in all would amount somewhere between $200,000 to $300,000," he shrugged.

"I tell you what Jr. why wait until then, if that's what you want, why don't I just write you out a check for $250,000 thousand and you won't have to worry about it, how's that," I asked in an angry tone.

"Naw, dad, it's not that, I'm just…"

"Jr. I think it's best that you leave my house now. I haven't been so disappointed in you in a very long time but today, today you have shown me that you only care about what I can give you," I stated sadly.

"Naw, dad I'm just…"

"Jr. leave my house now," I said standing up from my seat.

"Fine, I'll leave if that's what you want," he said raising his voice and walking pass me.

"Dad, we are so sorry that you had to go through that. But, Junior's heart is in the right place. He does love you," Valerie said trying to convince me.

"Well, that's a fine way to show it," I replied walking into my house and up my stairs.

I was so pissed I couldn't believe that Jr. would say something like that. "Hey Pop-pop, is everything alright," I heard Nicky stay as I walked by his room.

"Sure, everything is fine. Why you asked that," I asked standing in his doorway and watching him as he plays with his video game.

"Well, I heard big brother James and he didn't sound too happen," he answered sadly.

"Look," I began as I came in his room and sat next to him on his bed. "Jr. doesn't really mean what he says most of the time. Unfortunately, he doesn't always think before he speaks, you know?"

"That's how my big sister Rasheeda is," he smiled.

"Is that right, why would you say that?"

"Well, I promised Rasheeda I wouldn't tell," he said lowering his head.

"Ok, secrets are important to keep but there not always good to keep if someone might get hurt as a result of that secret. Do you understand?"

"Yes," he replied nodding his head up and down.

"So, I want you to know that you can tell me anything, ok?"

"Well, Saturday at the cookout, I overheard my sister Rasheeda and that lady name Ms. Angela talking."

"Well, you know it's not nice to ease drop on people's conversation. You know that right?"

"I wasn't trying to, I wanted to use the bathroom and they were in there for the longest time. So, I waited outside the door until they were through. Once they came out, they didn't know I was there and my sister Rasheeda told me not to say one word of anything I heard."

"Well, Nicky, if it's something that can hurt someone I think you need to let me know."

"But I don't wanna get anybody in trouble and I promised Rasheeda," he said lowering his head.

"Ok, well, I'm here if and when you wanna talk about it. I hope you realize that you can tell me anything and that I love you. I'm here to nurture you and protect you as my own, you understand?"

"Ok, well if I tell you, you won't tell anybody I told you, would you," he asked looking up at me.

"Of course not."

"Well, I didn't hear all of what they said but Ms. Angela was talking to Rasheeda about raising a newborn and that it wasn't easy. And Rasheeda asked her about the baby daddy and Ms. Angela said that she didn't know who her baby daddy was. And that confused me because I know Cousin Terry is Ms. Angela's baby daddy, right?"

Out of the mouths of babes, I thought to myself. Nicky shocked me so that I don't know what bothered me the most my son complaining about his inheritance or Terry possibly not being Angela's baby daddy.

Although, Angela doesn't know Rasheeda that well at all and maybe just she said that because she didn't want Rasheeda in her business.

I didn't want Nicky to feel bad about telling me about this so I just simply try to play it down by saying, "Well, Nicky, maybe you just misunderstood what she said. Besides we all know that's Terry's baby, right," I said grabbing him and tickling him.

§§§§§

Terry

"Unc, had me thinking a lot today about my situation with Angela," I said to Frankie as we lye in each other's arms.

"What you mean, you guys didn't get any work done."

"Yeah we did but he also told me that he

spoke with Angela and she's actually thinking about taking me to court so that we can share in the custody of Brittany."

"What, are you serious," he asked leaning up from the bed.

"I wish I wasn't."

"So, what are you going to do?"

"Don't you mean, what are we going to do," I rephrased as I leaned over and kissed him on the mouth.

"Ok, ok, what are we going to do," he smiled.

"To be honest, I wish we could just raise her as our own. I mean, I see gay guys do that all the time. As a matter of fact, I saw this one clip on facebook with these 2 guys combing their daughter's hair and getting them ready for school and now all of a sudden, the video went viral and now they're famous.

"Oh yeah, I saw that video. Those brothas were hot too," he laughed.

"Ok Frankie, focus, a'ight," I replied slapping him on his booty.

"Well, it would be nice but there's a problem," he said looking at me strangely.

"What's the problem," I shrugged.

"You haven't told anybody you're gay, duh!"

"Oh yeah," I laughed.

"Oh yeah, hell, you need to come out the closet and be who you are," he scoffed.

"I know you're right. I just don't know how Unc would take it. I mean, I've been a womanizer for so long," I laughed grabbing my manhood.

"Chile boo," I'm sure James wouldn't have a problem with it at all. Hell, he's gay, we're all gay, except for Angela and I sometimes worry about her, ok?"

"Ok, so how about this weekend we take Unc out for dinner or something and tell him about us as well as to see if he can talk Angela into letting us raise Brittany ourselves?"

"Really, are you serious," he asked being all excited and shit.

"Yes, really."

"Well, in that case, I think you deserve some special love making tonight," Frankie said as he pulled out the play handcuffs in the nightstand and then told me to close my eyes.

Chapter 7

Juan

It's been almost a whole week and I have
not heard from Ken since last Saturday when I
dropped him home from James's cookout
celebration. I know Ken sometimes get in his
little moods but I've been calling and texting
him all week and not once has he returned any
of my calls. I have begun to worry. I mean
with Ken's health problems, anything can
happen, you know?

Since Ken hasn't called me, I wonder if
anyone else has heard from him. Its 9:45,
good, James should be at work by now. I
picked up my office phone and dialed his
number.

"Good morning, this is James L. Parker Attorney at Law office. How can I help you," Sherry said answering the phone.

"Hey Sherry, this is Juan, is James around?"

"Sure hold on, I'll get him on the line for you."

"Thank you."

After a moment or two, James came on the line, "Hey you, how's your Friday morning going thus far? I'm sure your fast tail probably got plans for the weekend already, huh," he laughed into the phone.

"Actually I don't. I was calling you to see if you had heard from Ken?"

"Naw, I hadn't heard or seen Ken since my cookout last Saturday. Wow, this is kind of unlike Ken not to stay in touch."

"Well, I know for a fact, he does get in his moods at times and I'm just wondering if this is one of those times," I said being concern.

"I tell you what, hold on and I'll get

Angela and Frankie on the phone and we can conference call."

"Oh ok cool, I know your office do have one of those fancy hook-ups with the phone line," I laughed.

"Hold on," he said as I heard several buttons being pushed on his end.

A couple minutes went by and James clicked over and said, "Hey Juan, you still there?"

"Yes."

"Ok, cool because I have Angela and Frankie on the line as well."

"Good morning guys," I said.

"Hey Juan," both Angela and Frankie said in unison. "So, what's going on," Angela asked.

"Well, I hope nothing is going on but have either one of you heard from Ken," I asked nervously.

"Naw, I hadn't seen or heard from Ken since the cookout," Frankie stated.

"Neither have I," Angela chimed in.

"Do you think something is wrong,"

Frankie asked.

"I'm not sure," I said again while becoming worried.

"What does that mean," James asked.

"I mean nothing really except when I dropped him home from the cookout, he said that he wanted to tell me something but then changed his mind," I confessed.

"What and you didn't force him to tell you, like you always do," James laughed.

"Naw, not this time besides, I was tired and he was tired so I just wanted to go home a crash, you know," I stated.

"So, have you tried going over to his house," Angela asked.

"No, I haven't but I'll definitely do that once I get off of work today."

"I'm sure everything is ok, you know Ken, he probably cooped up in his place with a piece, you know what I'm saying," Frankie laughed.

"Oh, wait, hold on my cell, that might be him," I said placing them on hold. "Hello," I said answering my cell phone.

"Hey," I heard Ken whispered into the phone.

"Man, where are you? You know I've been calling and texting you all week and you haven't returned any of my calls," I asked angrily.

"Look, stop fussing alright and I'll tell you," he whispered into the phone.

"And why are you whispering," I asked being annoyed.

"I'm in the hospital and I've been here since Monday morning. Can you please come pick me up," he asked above a whispered.

"In the hospital," I almost shouted.

"Look, can you come get me or not," Ken whispered.

"Well of course, what hospital?"

"Carolinas Medical Center off of Blythe Blvd."

"Ok fine, I'll be there as soon as I can."

"Thank you," he whispered.

"Hey, I have the gang on the phone you want us all to come?"

"No, just you and don't open your big mouth and tell them I'm in the hospital, either," he insisted.

"Why not, we are a family you know?"

"Please Juan, just come alone," he begged.

"Ok, fine, I'll be there as soon as I can. I'm leaving now."

"Thank you," he replied and hung up.

"Hey, you guys still there," I asked taking them off of hold.

"Well dayum, I thought you forgot all about us," James laughed.

"It must have been some hot piece," Angela scoffed.

"Was that Ken," James asked.

"Ah, no, ah, it was a damn bill collector and you know how they are," I said trying to be as convincing as I could.

"Ah, no darling, I don't know how they can be," Angela hissed.

"Chile Boo, anyway, I gotta go but I will stop by Ken's house when I get off and I'll let y'all know what's going on, ok," I asked hanging up the phone before either one of them could respond.

§§§§§

In less than an hour later I was walking into Carolinas Medical Center. I stopped by the information desk, gave the clerk Ken's information and was informed that he was in room 412. The clerk gave me a visitor's pass and I found the closet elevator. Once I reached the 4th floor, I went looking for room 412. Once I found it, I walked in and noticed that Ken was sitting in the chair, fully clothed and his bag pack was lying on the bed.

"What in the hell is going on with you," I asked while sitting on the side of the bed facing him.

"Could you be a little nicer? I don't know if you noticed or not, but I've been sick, you know," he replied looking around the room for emphasis.

"Ok, I'm sorry. What's going on, Ken, you had me worried."

"Well, remember last Saturday when you took me home and I said I had something to tell you?"

"Yes."

"Well, I really didn't want to say anything at the time because I had a doctor's appointment that Monday and I wanted to wait for my test results before saying anything to anybody," he replied choking up.

"What test results," I asked sadly.

"Well, along with the back problems I've been having, I'm also HIV positive and the medication that I'm taking for both seem not to work together," he answered as water build up in his eyes.

"HIV positive? How, what, I mean, you just found this out?"

"No Juan, I've known for almost 10 years. You know my lover died from AIDS and I never said anything about it but I had contracted the virus from him," he answered wiping the tears from his eyes.

"Wow, Ken, I'm so sorry my brotha," I said as I stood and kneeled in front of him. "I wish you would have told me."

"I didn't want to. I didn't want anyone to know. I mean, Juan I'm 52 years old, I'm not supposed to be HIV positive, I'm too old for that," he replied angrily.

"Look Ken, being HIV positive has nothing to do with how old you are. Anybody can become infected," I said trying to assure him in some way.

"I know that Juan, but I'm just not ready to accept it or admit to it but now, I don't have a choice," he said looking at me in my eyes.

"Why, what's wrong," I asked nervously.

"The reason why I was here was for them to change my medication and see if that would work."

"And."

"It doesn't seem to be working."

"So, what does that mean?"

"There's nothing else they can do," he replied again choking up.

I don't know what to say or how to feel about this whole situation. I know that I need to be understanding and supportive but for right now, I'm pissed. Out of all of us, Ken and I have been friends the longest and we have been through so many ups and downs that it's not even funny. We have shared men together, we have cried together, we've celebrated Christmas's, birthdays, Thanksgiving, everything and yet, he keeps this from me. I know it's not about me but I'm angry.

§§§§§

Ken received his departure papers from the hospital and I drove him home. There wasn't much said on the ride home because I was so angry, I didn't want to have an accident. So, I kept my thoughts to myself until I got Ken home safely.

Once we made it inside Ken's home, I couldn't hold it any longer. "You know what," I said raising my voice while entering his home.

"Excuse you," he replied looking at me strangely.

"You are a selfish son-of-a-bitch, you know that," I said getting up in his face.

"What are you talking about," he replied walking away from me and sitting down on his living room couch.

"You heard what I said, you are a selfish son-of-a-bitch," I said standing over him.

"And how you figure that," he said becoming agitated.

"You have been sick this long and today you decide to tell me about your illness, really, Ken," I said as I began to pace his living room floor.

"Well first of all, why are you making this

about you," he argued.

"I'm not making it about me. I'm making it about the close friendship I thought we had," I hissed.

"No, no you're not, you trying to make it about you because you always wanna know every dayum thing and some things you don't need to know," he said trying to raise his voice.

"Well if that was the case, then why in the hell you're telling me now," I said with my hands on my hips.

"That's a good question as a friend I thought you would be a little more understanding and supportive but all I'm getting from you is how you feel and not about how I feel," he answered standing up from the couch.

"See, here you go with that woo is me mentality. Always looking for sympathy and telling people, I've been sick, you know. You pull that shit all the time. Even when we both were seeing homeboy and he left you and began seeing me. You got mad because he choose me and you couldn't stand it and like always, you went into this woo is me act."

"Woo is me act, what the fuck are you talking about, woo is me, act? Bitch, I don't have to act or surrender to some woo is me mentality. Your ass just wants to be in everybody's business and you're upset because you just see it as "Dirt" and try to use it against me at some point," he argued.

"Use it against you? All the shit we've been through and all that I already know about your stank ass, chile boo," I replied rolling my neck at him.

"See, that's why I didn't tell you because I knew you would probably throw it up in my face, or at least tell James considering you tell him every dayum thing anyway," he said rolling his neck back at me.

"You know what, Ken, FUCK YOU," I yelled.

"Fuck you too and as a matter of fact, why don't you get the fuck out of my house," he said trying to holler back at me.

"Fine, you gonna need me before I need you," I replied walking to his front door.

"Whatever, bitch."

"Back atchoo bitch," I replied opening his front door and slamming it behind me.

Chapter 8

James

Thank God I made it through another week. All I can say is, "Thank God it's Friday," I said to myself as I pulled off and on my way to pick up Nicky from summer camp.

As much as I am glad that the weekend is here, I am concern about Terry. Apparently he has some things on his mind that he wants to discuss with me. In the past, when Terry wants to talk or discuss something it hasn't always been good news. So I am on pens and needles because I don't know what's been going on with him. I guess I'll find out tonight. Terry wanted to take me out to dinner but I suggested that he comes over to my place and have a pizza and movie night with me and Nicky.

I pulled right in front of Nicky's summer camp building and saw him standing outside with some of the other kids who were waiting for their parents to pick them up along with Ms. Richardson. All I can say about her is that if I was straight, she could get it and if I was 30 years younger, I would take it. Anyway, I beeped my horn and Nicky turn around and came running over to my car and got in. Ms. Richardson waved as I drove by.

"So, how was your day at summer camp," I asked starting conversation.

"It was cool, they taught us how to swim today," he replied with excitement.

"Oh yeah."

"Yeah, it was fun."

"So, you know what tonight is?"

"It's Friday, pizza and movie night," he yelled with excitement.

"Yup, it sure is but I just wanted you to know that cousin Terry would be joining us. Is that ok?"

"Oh ok, Cousin Terry is funny, I like him because he makes me laugh," he smiled.

"Well, Cousin Terry can be a hoot," I smiled.

"A hoot, what's that?"

"It's a person that can make you laugh. We call them a hoot," I explained.

"Hmmm, I like that," he replied while giving it some thought. "I have to use that when he comes over."

"Haha, you do that." I looked over at him

and asked, "So, now that your big brother and big sisters have gone back home, and it's just us, how do you feel about that?"

"Well, as much as I enjoyed Michelle and Valerie, I hated to see them leave last night but Big brother Junior, not so much," he said shaking his head from side to side.

"Well, remember I told you, big brother Junior means well he just doesn't think about the things he says before saying them."

"He just doesn't like me," he said lowering his head.

"That's not true, I know he likes you a lot it's just that he has been the only boy in the family for a long time. He just has to get use to having a little brother, that's all."

§§§§§

Once we got home, I had Nicky put his things away, take a quick shower and put on his pajamas so we could chill out in the living room, eat Pizza and watch movies.

The pizza guy dropped off 3 large cheese Pizzas, a large order of hot wings and a 2 liter of coke. Before I could even set everything up in the living room, there was a knock on the door. I knew it must have been Terry.

"Hey Unc, I can smell the pizza all the way out here," Terry said as I opened the door to let him in. However, to my surprise he wasn't alone. He brought Frankie with him.

"Hey Frankie, this is a surprise," I said giving him a brotherly hug.

"Hey Cousin Terry, you know what," Nicky asked.

"What's that little man," Terry asked kneeling down to give him a hug.

"You're a hoot," Nicky said as he cracked up laughing.

"Oh Lawd, Unc must have told you that, didn't he?"

"Yup," Nicky said laughing while shooting

me under the bus.

"Hey Nicky, it's nice to see you. How's school," Frankie asked.

"Uncle Frankie, this is summer time, there's no school. Don't you know that," Nicky asked looking at Frankie with a strange expression on his face. "You mean summer camp."

"Well, excuse me it's been a minute since I've been in school. So, how is summer camp," Frankie asked correcting himself.

"Look, can we all just take a seat in the living room and eat before these pizzas get cold," I asked.

I grabbed several paper plates out of the kitchen and we all sat in the living room, eating our pizza, talking, and cracking jokes on one another. I still didn't know why Terry wanted to talk to me or why Frankie was with him but for the time being we were having fun and that's all that mattered.

"So Unc, whatever happened to that book you were writing? It's been almost a year and I hadn't heard you say anything about it."

"Well, it takes a minute to write a book, I'm still working on it. It's just that I've been kind of busy with work and looking after Nicky," I confessed.

"Naw, it ain't that, you just getting old," Terry said as he and Nicky both laughed.

"Well, I don't know about that. Although it's getting harder for me to stand up from a chair or sit down in one without making noise," I said laughing at myself.

"And when was the last time you been to a thrift store? I know that's what old people do. They like shopping at the thrift stores," Frankie asked as he looked around to see if I had brought anything new or in this case, used.

"See, that's another thing. You young people call it shopping but when you get to my age, we call it plundering," I answered as they looked at me and laughed.

"Plunder, dayum I gotta remember that," Terry said as he continued to laugh.

Several hours later as we continued to discuss the difference of what old people do versus what younger people do, I noticed Nicky had had enough and had fallen asleep on the floor. "Look guys, I'll be right back. I'm going to put Nicky to bed, a'ight?"

"Ok, we'll be here," Frankie replied as he got up to clean the mess we made.

Terry

"You know bae, I'm a little nervous about telling Unc about us," I stated while helping Frankie with the mess we made.

"I know, I see you sweating already," he said looking at me and laughing.

"But if this means being able to raise my daughter, Brittany, I'm willing to do that."

"So we can raise her, you mean," he

corrected.

"You know that's what I meant. See how nervous I am?"

"Ok gentlemen, where were we," James asked as he came back out into the living room.

"Well Unc, I just wanted to tell you something but it's kind of hard for me to say it."

"Well, I find that when you have something to say to someone and it's hard to do, the best thing to do is just spit it out," he said in an encouraging way.

"Well, I know you probably have been wondering what I've been doing since Angela and I are no longer seeing one another," I began.

"The thought has crossed my mind," Unc stated.

"Well, it's like this," I said swallowing and taking a deep breath. "I've been hanging out with Frankie," he replied looking over at Frankie.

"Okay, hanging out, meaning what exactly?"

"You know, Unc," I replied shrugging my shoulders for effect.

"No, I don't know."

"Look James, your nephew is gay and we are lovers," Frankie blurted out.

"I was gonna tell him, dayum," I said looking over at Frankie.

"Well, you were taking too dayum long for me, so?"

"I see," Unc said leaning back on the couch and looking at the both of us.

"Is that all you have to say," I asked.

"What else do you want me to say?"

"I dunno, something to at least show you care."

"Terry I do care, you know I love you like you're my son. I'm just kind of surprise considering you've been chasing after older women since you got your first piece of pussy, what 15 or 16?"

"14 actually," I smiled with pride.

"Whatever," Unc replied.

"Look James, I know this must come as a surprise to you but Terry and I do love each other," Frankie informed.

"Is that right," he asked looking over at me.

"Yes Unc, I do," I admitted.

"So, what now, why is it important that you guys tell me now?"

"Well first of all, you are my Uncle and you and Frankie have been friends for a good while and also because you are an attorney," I stated.

"What does me having to be an attorney got to do with you being gay," Unc questioned.

"Well Unc, the other day when you mentioned about Angela taking me to court to share custody I thought why not take her to court to get full custody and me and Frankie can raise her ourselves."

"Oh really?

"Ah, yeah, really," I replied.

"Ok, well I'm not that kind of lawyer,

remember?"

"I know Unc but I thought you would know a little something about child welfare or whatever it's called."

"Well first, you have to establish you have rights. Did you sign the birth certificate when Brittany was born?"

"No," I replied looking down at the floor.

"Why not," Unc asked.

"I didn't know that Angela had even had the baby until afterwards and remember, you were the one that called and told me."

"So, James, what you're saying is Terry needs to partition the court for a DNA test in order to claim parental rights," Frankie asked.

"Exactly."

"Well Unc, is it something I can do myself or do I need a lawyer?"

"As far as petitioning the courts you can do that yourself. You don't need to hire a lawyer for that."

"Ok, well, I'll do that first thing Monday morning considering we will be down at the courthouse anyway."

"Now, you sure you want to do that," Unc asked.

"Yes."

"Ok, but you know Angela is my friend and I don't really want to be a part of it. We can get all the forms you need on Monday morning but I'm not going to help you fill them out. You're going to have to do that on your own, you understand?"

"I understand and thanks, Unc."

"Don't thank me because you know how Angela is and she is going to jump all in your shit. I'm just saying," he laughed.

"Well, I guess she'll just have to jump in my shit as well," Frankie stated.

"Oh, trust me, I'm sure she will," Unc said cracking up.

Chapter 9

Angela
3 weeks later

"Good morning Ms. Dobson, you have a special delivery letter that just came for you. I placed it on your desk in your office," my secretary, Teresa said as I walked by her desk to enter my office.

"Thank you Teresa. Oh, can you get me a cup of coffee? I've been up all night with the baby and I didn't get much sleep at all," I asked while sitting down at my desk.

"Sure, no problem."

I picked up the big vanilla envelope and notice that it was from the Juvenile

Courthouse here in Charlotte. "What the hell," I said to myself. I opened the envelope and pulled out a petition that Terry was filing to get a DNA test done on Brittany. "No his trifling ass didn't," I said to myself.

"Here's your coffee Ms. Dobson," Teresa said as she walked in my office and placed the cup of coffee in front of me.

"I can't believe this son-of-a-bitch," I said still looking at the petition.

"Is something wrong Ms. Dobson?"

"My no good baby daddy is what's wrong," I scoffed.

"Join the club, I got one of those too," Teresa said shaking her head from side to side.

"Maybe so, but your baby daddy isn't petitioning the courts for a DNA test, is he?"

"No, he better not," she hissed and then looked at me side eyed as though there was so doubt as to who my baby daddy is.

"That will be all," Teresa," I said with a little attitude.

I wonder who put his no good ass up to this, I thought to myself. I hope James wouldn't do something like this even though blood is thicker than water or so they say. James must have done something because terry is too stupid to even know how to petition anything when it comes to anything legal. I picked up my phone and called James.

"Mr. Parker's office, can I help you?"

"Good morning Sherry, this is Angela, is James available?"

"Good moring, hold on for a sec and I'll see, ok," she replied putting me on hold.

"Hey you," James said answering the phone all chipper and shit.

"Don't hey me, James. What's going on with your nephew," I spat.

"Oh, I see, you must have gotten the petition papers from the courts."

"Yes, I did and whose idea was this?"

"Hey look, he said he wanted to verify that Brittany was his for sure. I had nothing to do with that other than show him the papers he would have to fill out at the courthouse."

"So, he trying to say I'm a hoe or something and that I don't know who my baby father is," I said becoming angry.

"Wait a minute, hold on Angela, I don't think it's that but you should talk to him about this. Like I told him from the beginning I didn't want to be placed in the middle."

"I understand that, but you couldn't give me a heads-up?"

"No Angela because like I said, I don't want to be in the middle."

"Ok, fine. I'm sorry James, I'm not mad at you. I'm just pissed at your nephew," I sighed.

"Apology accepted. So how is baby girl?"

"She's fine but won't let a sista get a full night of sleep for nothing."

"Awe, brings back memories," he laughed.

"Oh shut up. I gotta run I will call you later, smooches."

James

I knew Angela wasn't going to be too happy about that at all. "Hey Sherry, is Terry out there," I asked yelling out into the outer office.

"He went to Office Depot to get some supplies, remember? He should be back in minute now."

"Oh, ok, well when he comes back, will you let him know I would like to see him?"

"Ok, will do."

§§§§§

Juan

You know it's a damn shame that the older we get the more suborned we get. I haven't heard from Ken since our last argument and that's been almost 3 weeks ago. Truth is, I haven't reached out to him either and I do feel bad about it.

Ken has always been my ride or die kind of friend for almost 25 years. There is so much that we have been through that for something like this to happen and we don't speak to one another for weeks at a time is ridiculous.

I've said some not so nice things to him and he has said some not so nice things to me but I guess the bottom line is that friends go through their ups and downs like any other kind of relationship.

What's so interesting is that Ken had seriously been on my mind since last night. I couldn't sleep at all and I started to call him and pretty much beg him for his forgiveness but being stubborn, I didn't. Maybe I'll stop by his house once I get off from work today. Hell, I should just leave now considering my mind really isn't focused on anything but Ken.

Just at that moment when I had decided to leave work early, my cell phone began to ring. I looked down at the number but I didn't recognize it. "Hello," I said hesitantly.

"Ah, yes, is this Mr. Johnson," the caller asked.

"Yes, it is and who am I speaking to?"

"This is Doctor Saunders at Carolinas Medical Center. I'm Mr. Hutchins physician. We met the last time you had come to pick him up and take him home."

"Oh yes, I remember you now. Well tell Ken that I am actually leaving work now, so if he's there, I can come and pick him up," I said gathering my things.

"Well sir, I don't think that would be necessary. I was calling to see if you knew his next of kin?"

"His next of kin, what you mean? Is there something wrong?"

"Well, I'm really not allowed to go into that but I would like to talk to his next of kin if you know who that might be?"

"His next of kin is me. Ken is my life

partner," I said lying.

"Oh, I didn't know. Well, I hate to be the one to tell you but Mr. Hutchins past away in his sleep early this morning."

"Excuse me, what did you say," I asked not believing what he just told me.

"Mr. Hutchins past away in his sleep early this morning."

My cell phone slipped out of my hand and fell to the floor. I stood there in shock for at least several minutes not feeling a thing. And suddenly, the tears gushed out of my eyes like a waterfall. I couldn't believe my best friend in the world had died on me.

"Mr. Johnson, are you ok," one of my co-workers walked over and asked.

"It's not fair, it's just not fair," is all I could say as the tears continued to flow.

"Why don't you have a seat," my co-worker stated as he helped me sit down at my desk. "Would you like some water or something?"

"I gotta get outta here, I gotta get outta here," I kept saying as I grabbed my things and practically ran out of my office not knowing where I was going or how I was getting there.

§§§§§

Terry

"Hey Unc, you busy," I said peaking my head into his office. "Sherry said you wanted to see me."

"Yes, I do. Come in and have a seat," Unc stated not sounding to cheerful.

"Is something wrong," I asked sitting down.

"I don't know but, I just got a call from Angela. She is in receipt of the petition you filed and she is not happy," he answered while sitting back in his chair.

"Good, I'm glad, fuck her," I said angrily.

"Look Terry, I told you I didn't want to get in the middle of this. I love the both of you and I don't want to be put in a position whereby I would have to choose sides. That's not fair to me."

"I know Unc but for the past few weeks, she hasn't allowed me to see my daughter or anything. So, at this point I'm fed up, you feel me?"

"No, I don't feel you. I wish you young folks quit saying that. However, if you are as fed up as you claim to be, I suggest that you act like an adult and communicate how you feel with her."

"Well Unc, I would be at this point, I think it's too late. I mean, now that she got the petition I'm sure I'm the last person she would want to talk to. Besides, I want the court's to handle it and being that she's an attorney, I believe that's the only way to get through to her," I sighed.

"Hmmm, I guess you have a point. What is the date that you guys have to appear in court?"

"Well, next Wednesday is the day we have to take the DNA test and the following Monday is when we appear in court. Will you be able to attend the hearing?"

"Yes, I will be there but I want you to understand that I'll be there in support of both of you regardless what the results are, do you understand?"

"Yeah, Unc, I feel you, I mean I understand," I replied smiling and walking out of his office.

Chapter 10

Juan

Once I left my office and got in my car, I realized one thing to be true that Ken said to me, "You always make things about you!" As much as it hurts, it was true; I do try to make things about me.

I wiped the tears from my eyes, pulled myself together and drove down to Carolinas Medical Center to see my dear friend and to say goodbye.

It's funny, I found myself laughing at all the memories that Ken and I shared together. But, there was none funnier than when he hurt himself at work and had a piano fall on him. I know one shouldn't laugh at someone's pain but in time, even Ken had to laugh about it.

I remember after him being in the hospital for almost a month, once he got out, he would tell anybody that would listen about him being in the hospital and saying. "I've been sick, you know?" It doesn't sound as funny now just thinking about it but I guess it's one of those things of, you had to be there.

Ken had a wonderful sense of humor he could make anyone laugh no matter how down they might be. Ken would look you dead in the eye and say, "I've been sick, you know?" Of course he was still saying this many years later. But sure enough, it made us laugh. I guess Ken got the last laugh. I know I'm going to miss my old friend.

§§§§§

Once I got to the hospital, I asked to speak to Ken's physician, Doctor Saunders. He escorted me into a small room right outside the waiting room and offered me a seat.

"I'm glad you were able to come down so quickly Mr. Johnson," he stated.

"Why wouldn't I, I mean, what happened?"

"Mr. Hutchins had come back to the hospital about a week ago and he's been here ever since. The medication that we had given him seemed to have been too much for his body to take. I explained to Mr. Hutchins that this medication was the last resort and if his body wouldn't accept it, he would die."

"A week, are you serious," I asked lowering my head down to the floor.

"Yes, I thought you were aware."

"How could I be aware, had you seen me since the last time I was here," I replied becoming agitated.

"No, I hadn't but I am not able to contact anyone without Mr. Hutchins permission and I as well as the nurses constantly asked Mr. Hutchins if he would like us to call anyone for him and he kept saying, "No.""

"Can I see him," I asked as the tears began to well up in my eyes.

"Sure, he's still in his room. I knew you were coming and I didn't want them to move him down to the morgue just yet.

I followed Doctor Saunders out of the room and down the hallway to Ken's room. As I opened the door, Doctor Saunders said, "I will give you some privacy and I'll be right outside the door if you need anything."

"Thank you," I whispered as I slowly entered the room and stood over my dear friend.

Truth is, Ken didn't look dead at all. As a matter of fact, I was waiting for him to open his eyes and shout, "Ah hi, Gotcha," but he didn't. Although, I wished he had.

I pulled up a chair next to his bed and began talking to him. "Ken, I guess you got the last laugh after all, huh? Wow man, what am I going to do without you? See, there I go thinking about me again. You were right about that as well. Ken, if you can hear me, I want you to know that I've always loved you like a brother and there was nothing in this world I would not have done for you," I had to stop at this point because I could no longer control the tears and snot that flew out of my body. I looked around for some tissues or a towel so that I could blow my nose and wipe my face.

After finding some tissue in the bathroom, I sat back down and continued talking to my friend. "Remember that time, I guess it was about 20 years ago that we both dressed up in drag for Halloween," I asked laughing. "We looked a hot mess, I don't know who looked worse, me or you.

"And if you told another person about your hospital story and saying, "I've been sick, you know," I personally was gonna punch you in the throat. "I guess I have to contact your family and let them know. And forgive me for lying and telling the doctor we were lovers, that was the only way that I knew they would let me see you. I haven't told any of the gang just yet. I'm not even sure how I would say it. And even though we all have had our ups and downs we all are going to miss you, even Frankie."

I had to laugh because Frankie and Ken never really got along. I think that even though we all were older than Frankie, I think Ken had a thing for Frankie but Frankie would never accept any of Ken's passes.

"Anyway Ken, I love you man and always will. I hope and pray that wherever you are, you're no longer in pain and that you are happy. Oh, and tell my momma and daddy that I said hello and I love and miss them every day. And don't worry about a thing my friend; I will make sure you go out in grand style."

I stood up and leaned over and kissed Ken on the forehead, "Sleep well Ken, I hope to see you again one day. I love you, man."

I walked out of the hospital feeling so alone, so pissed, so frustrated and in despair. I didn't know where I was going and I didn't know what time it was. All I remember is that walked around the hospital in a daze for hours.

§§§§§

James

"Excuse me Mr. Parker, I think Juan is on the other line and wants to speak with you," Sherrie my secretary said walking into my office.

"What do you mean, you think it's Juan? Don't you know his voice by now," I chuckled.

"Yeah I do but he seemed to be crying," she replied while handing me the phone.

"Hello, Juan are you ok?"

"No, not really," he said sniffling into the phone.

"Why, what's wrong?"

"I'm down here at Carolinas Medical Center," he began and then started to choke up.

"What's going on, are you ok, were you in n accident or something," I asked becoming concern.

"No James, I'm fine. It's Ken," again he sniffled into the phone.

"What about Ken, is he ok?"

"Naw, James, Ken is not ok, not this time," he replied sadly.

"What do you mean," I asked not wanting to hear the worse.

"He's gone, James, Ken is gone," Juan said in almost a whisper.

"Oh my God, no," I responded being in shock.

"Yes, its' true and I don't know what…"

"Look, I'm on my way down there. Don't do anything yet, I'll handle it."

"Hurry James, hurry," Juan said as I could

hear the pain in his cry.

Chapter 11

Juan

Ken's Funeral

The sanctuary wasn't as full as I thought it would be as I looked around and noticed some people I hadn't seen in years. I was able to reach Ken's family and they pretty much put the funeral together because truth is, I couldn't. I know it's not about me but I am still hurting to the point where I can hardly think straight.

Ken's sister Margaret did a beautiful job in arranging the entire service. I was given the liberty to pick out Ken's suit. I knew Ken always looked sharp and nothing was too good or too expensive for my friend's "Going Home Service."

I brought Ken a black Italian, wide, notch lapel, 2 piece suit and I have to admit, he was looking sharper than a mosquito's peeder as us old folks used to say. Margaret knew Ken and I were very close and therefore she allowed me to say a few words on behalf of his friends.

I sat there with James on one side of me and Angela on the other side as we held hands for support of one another and Terry and Frankie sat behind us. "And right now, we will have a few words from Mr. Hutchins dearest friend, Mr. Juan Johnson," I heard the pastor say.

I rose from my seat and walked my way up to the pulpit and stood behind the microphone. My nerves were getting the best of me because my hands were sweaty and my knees were shaking. I took a deep breath and looked down at Ken's coffin and then out into the audience and I began, "Ken used to always tell people that he had been in the hospital and say, I've been sick, you know!" Those of us that knew Ken, and have heard his hospital story all broke out in laughter.

"I know most of you might think I'm crazy but I actually saw and had a conversation with Ken a couple of nights ago." I noticed people in the audience turned their heads and looked at one another as though they really thought I had lost it, but I didn't care. So I continued, "What was funny is that when I saw Ken he looked exactly the same way he looked the day I met him all those years ago. Who knew death could make you look so good," I smiled to myself. "But I asked Ken, why did you leave me? He said, his name was called, and I was like, your name was called, who called your name? He told me God called his name. Well, I don't know about y'all but I was glad that I sometimes went to church, prayed and paid my tithes because this was the first time that I really realize there was a God, my best friend came back from death and told me."

"I told Ken that I was asked to speak at his funeral and I didn't know what I was going to say. So, I asked him, what do you want me to say? He looked me dead in the eyes and said, be honest and speak from the heart. I felt my eyes water when he said that. But then, it seemed as though he was about to float away but I had one more question and I said, Ken, he looked down at me and I said why in the world you would always tell people that you've been in the hospital and then tell them, I've been sick you know? As though you wore being sick a badge of honor or that you were proud to be sick. He simply said, I wasn't saying it because I was proud I was sick, I was saying it because I was proud that God healed me, like he always have, even now.

"Here again, I found myself getting upset with my friend because he said that God had even healed him now and all I could do was yell, NO HE DIDN'T. And Ken said looking down at me with a smile on his face and said, YES HE DID."

I had to take a moment to get myself together because I was so choke up that I thought, I won't and can't cry for Ken, I refuse to because I know where ever he is, he's doing just fine.

And then I continued, "What most of you guys don't know is that Ken saved my life. When we met, I was into some serious drugs at that time and Ken took the time to help me get the help that I needed. My own family wasn't there for me but Ken was. It was hard and there were times when I thought I hated him because he was making me do something I didn't want or like and that was to get clean. Six months later I became clean and have been for over 25 years, thanks to this brotha right here," I said looking down at Ken's coffin. "I never even said, thank you to him."

"Ken was my best friend in the entire world, we were closer then brothers. I must confess that about a month ago when he had gone into the hospital and he called and asked me to give him a ride home, I did but I was angry. I was so angry with Ken for not telling me that he was in the hospital that Ken and I literary cussed each other out that day. He told me that it wasn't about me but it was about him. It took me a minute to realize that but he was right. The worse thing about this is that once I realized he was right, it was too late for me to do anything about it. The next time I heard anything about Ken was 3 weeks later when his doctor called and told me he had passed." I had to stop at that point because I had literarily lost my balance. Once I gained composure, I saw James coming up to the pulpit and stood behind me with his arm around my left shoulder for support.

"I guess the morale to this story is, don't wait too late to tell someone you love them or that you're sorry because you never know when your time is up." I looked down at

Ken's coffin and said, "I love you old friend and I'm going to miss you like crazy. And for the record, I am so very sorry my friend and thank you so much for being a part of my life."

I turned and looked back at James to let him know I was finish and he helped me down from the pulpit and we both walked over and stood in front of Ken's coffin. "Goodbye my friend, I know one day we will see each other again," I whispered as I leaned over and placed the side of my head against Ken's closed coffin, hoping that God would bless me one more time and allow Ken to hear me.

§§§§§

After the service I didn't want to go to the burial ground or to the re-pass. So, the gang and I went over to James's house just to chill and talk about the good times and memories we had of Ken.

"Wow Juan, that was really nice what you said at the funeral, man," Terry said complimenting me.

"Yes, Juan, I was so very proud of you but at one point, look like you were going to break down so you know I had to come up there just in case, " James laughed.

"Thanks y'all, I appreciate that because I'm not into that public speaking thing, I'm just saying."

Unfortunately, as the time went on, the laughter came to an end because Angela and Terry got into it. I guess with everything that had been going on with me and Ken, I didn't know that Terry had filed a petition with the courts for a DNA test until Angela stood up from her chair and out of nowhere walked over to Terry and slapped the cowboy shit out of him and yelled, "How dare you take me to court for a DNA test. I know who the father of my child is, you Bastard."

But, that wasn't the worse of it because instead of Terry standing up and defending himself, of all people Frankie got up in Angela's face and said and I quote, "Don't be putting your hands on my man, hooka."

Now, I know it's not right to enjoy anyone's pain especially after coming from a funeral but I was blown away about Frankie's statement. And truth is, I know if Ken was here, he would have gotten a bag of popcorn and took a front seat because the drama was about to get real.

"Your man, what the fuck are you talking about," Angela asked rolling her neck with her hands on her hips.

"Bitch, you heard me, my man," Frankie stated again while rolling his neck back at her.

"Look you guys, y'all need to calm this down. We don't need to be acting like this especially after coming from Ken's funeral,"

James stated as he tried to get in between the two.

"I got your bitch aright," Angela hissed.

"James, you betta get her before I knock her ass out," Frankie said while trying to walk away from the situation.

"You ain't gonna do a damn thing you faggot ass mothafucka," Angela said raising her voice while trying to swing at Frankie.

Now again, this shit was funny as hell and I couldn't stop myself from laughing and I truly believe that Ken knew the pain in my heart and this was his way of cheering me up. Some would say that is a sick way of showing it but like I said, Ken had a sense of humor and sometimes it was kind of twisted.

"Yo Frankie, let's just go," Terry said getting up and trying to hold Frankie back.

"You betta get his ass," Angela shouted.

"Look Angela, you are not helping the situation. So, can we just go in the other room and talk like adults," James said trying to calm the situation.

"And for your information Ms. Thang, once the test come back and says that Terry is the father, we gonna take your ass back to court for full custody. What you gotta say about that heffa," Frankie yelled as Terry continued trying to get Frankie out of the house.

"If you think any court is going to take away my child and give it to a couple of faggots, you apparently don't know the law or me," Angela scoffed.

"Oh yeah, we'll see bitch," was the last thing Frankie said as Terry finally got him out of the house.

All I could say was, "Thanks Ken for the show, it was fabulous…"

Chapter 12

James

I will admit I grew up with the old saying, "Children should be seen and not heard." However, I also believe that children should learn as much about life as you can possibly teach them, especially about the laws in our society.

That being said today is the day of Terry and Angela's court results for the DNA test that Terry petition for. As I stated above, children should learn as much about life as well as our court system. What kind of father would I be if I didn't see to it that Nicky was informed about the law, especially me being an attorney?

Looking back on the situation I might not have brought him along if I knew things would turn out the way they did. But, I'll let you be the judge.

As Nicky and I sat in the court room waiting for the judge to enter, I tried pointing out various pictures that hung on the wall to Nicky. I explained the statue of a woman holding a candle but yet blind folded, indicating that justice is blind. I pointed out the gavel that laid on top of the judge's bench, letting Nicky know that when the judge pounds the gavel, that's for everyone in the courtroom to be quite.

"Hey Pop-pop," Nicky whispered leaning over close to me.

"Yeah."

"Did we do something wrong?"

"What do you mean?"

"That policeman keeps looking over at us," he stated as though he was scared.

I looked over and noticed this fine brotha in blue nodding his head and smiling at me.

Here again, how do you tell your 6 year old that this man likes me and is flirting with me?

In a way, the brotha was just my type and if Nicky had not been there with me, I probably would have gotten up from my seat and walked over to where he sat and give him one of my cards.

I just smiled and leaned over and said, "No Nicky, we didn't do anything wrong. The police officer is just being nice."

I looked about the courtroom and for some reason it was packed. I explained to Nicky that from where we sat, the plaintiffs stood on the right hand side and the defendants stood on the left hand side.

I saw both Terry and Frankie sitting up in the first row looking nervous as hell. I couldn't help but laugh to myself. I then looked over at Angela and noticed that she seemed to have been tied up looking through some papers that sat before her and on her cell phone. She didn't look happy at all, as a matter of fact, it looked as though she was fussing with someone on the other end.

"Here Ye, Here Ye, the court is now in session. The honorable Judge Randolph Alexander pre-siding," the bailiff yelled.

Everyone stood up in the courtroom as the judge made his way to his bench and stated, "Good morning everyone."

"Good morning," we said in unison.

"Before we begin, I want to warn you to turn off all electronic devices, phones, Ipads or whatever you might have."

People then began to turn their electronic devices off. I'm not sure if most people didn't already know this but as an attorney I always turn my off before I even walk into a courtroom.

"This courtroom is for the benefit of juvenile matters, along with custody issues as well as DNA testing. I ask everyone to respect my courtroom and only speak when spoken to, do you understand," the judge stated as he looked out into the courtroom. Most people said yes and nodded their heads.

"The first case on the docket Your Honor is Parker vs. Dobson, number 2567351," the bailiff said while giving the judge a vanilla folder.

"Well, Ms. Dobson, I'm surprise to see you in my courtroom today," the judge said looking over his bifocals at Angela.

"So am I Your Honor," Angela replied looking over at Terry and mean eyeing him.

"Mr. Parker, you filed a petition to have Ms. Dobson take a DNA test so that you can way parental rights for your child," the judge stated as he focused his attention on Terry.

"Yes, Your Honor," Terry said.

"Well, what happened, did you not signed your child's birth certificate when she was born," the judge asked.

"No Your Honor, I did not because I didn't

know that Angela…I mean, Ms. Dobson had the baby until after she was born Your Honor," Terry stated regrettably.

"So, Ms. Dobson, you didn't informed Mr. Parker that you had gone into labor with his child," the judge asked looking over at Angela.

"I did call him Your Honor, he never picked up his phone and I didn't leave a message."

"My I ask why," the judge asked.

"Your Honor, the man or shall I say boy, is just that, a boy. I don't have time to chase boys Your Honor. I'm not one of these women that chase any man. Mr. Parker knew I was pregnant and knew when my due date was. As a man, it's his responsibility to make sure his child is healthy and alive," Angela stated rolling her eyes over at Terry.

"Your Honor, the reason why she didn't tell me is that she got mad that I broke up with her stank ass…"

"Whoa, hold up young man. Like I said at the beginning you will respect my courtroom and the defendant as long as you're up in here. You understand?"

"I'm sorry Your Honor. I apologize.

"Is this true Ms. Dobson?"

"Your Honor, yes, we did break up but I wasn't mad about that. I was upset of the way he handle the situation."

"Ok Ms. Dobson. Well, you in turned had filed a petition to have another man take a DNA test for your daughter because you said that there could be a possibility of it being another man's child," the judge informed.

"Excuse me," Terry stated with attitude. "What the fuc…, sorry Your Honor, what do you mean it could be another man's child," Terry asked as I literally saw the steam coming from above his head.

I have to admit, I was very surprise that ultimately Angela didn't know who her baby daddy was and what Nicky had said to me about what he heard between Angela and Raheeda was true. Of course people were beginning to wake up and take notice in the case because it was having the same kind of drama we watch on TV.

My heart went out to Terry at this point because even though I didn't want to take sides, Angela had apparently been lying about Terry being the only man she had been with at that time of conception.

"Ms. Dobson, you have asked the courts not to name the other man for the sake of his own privacy. However, if Mr. Parker is not the father then and only then can we reveal the name of the other candidate who happens to be present in one of my rooms in the back.

"Yes Your Honor," Angela stated as she looked down to the floor.

"How could you do this to me," Terry blurted out while looking over at Angela.

"Young man, I've told you twice now, speak only when spoken to," the judge said looking at Terry.

"Again, I'm sorry Your Honor but you

have no idea what this woman have put me through and now to find out my daughter may not be mine, are you serious right," Terry asked as he rocked back and forth up at the podium.

I like said, Terry was pissed he couldn't keep still long enough to save his life, that's how upset he was. I looked over at Frankie and his jaw was almost on the floor. Truth is, I couldn't blame him either as I saw the shock on his face.

"Well, I'm really not here to get into you guys personal business. That's not what the court is for. We are here to establish parental rights and what's best for the child. Every child should and needs to know who their father is," the judge stated. "I have the results of the DNA test here for Mr. Parker, are you ready sir," the judge asked looking over his bifocals at Terry.

"Yes Your Honor," Terry stated as he

leaned on the podium to help keep him standing up.

The courtroom was quite so quite, you could hear a mouse pissing in the corner. That's how quite everything became as we all watched the judge open the envelope that would determine if Terry was the father or not.

"Well according to DNA Diagnostics, Mr. Parker I don't know if this is a good thing or not but, you are not the father."

"Seriously Angela, are you fucking serious," Terry yelled. "Who is the father, you bitch!"

For a minute I thought Terry was going to go completely off because as he started to walk over to where Angela stood, the bailiff immediately stood between them. Hell, even I stood up and went up front and stood next to Terry for support. I didn't want him to do anything that might cause him to get locked up and even though Angela might have deserved to be bitch slapped for that one, now was not the time.

"Bailiff, will you escort Mr. Parker out of my courtroom, please," the judge asked while banging his gavel on his desk. "Order in the court, order in the court."

A part of me wanted to get up and go out in the lobby and try to console my nephew but another part of me wanted to find out who the other man was who could possibly be the father of Angela's baby.

"Pop-pop, what happened? Cousin Terry isn't the father," Nicky asked while tugging on my shirt sleeve.

"It doesn't look like it Nicky, wow."

I then noticed that Frankie had gotten up and went out into the lobby. So, I felt at least someone would try to console him not knowing what Terry might have done. I can only imagine how devastating this must be for him to think you have a child one minute and then the next minute being told that you don't.

I would have never guessed that Terry wasn't the father. You see, in my family we have very strong genes when it comes to our eyes. My Aunt on my mother's side of the family used to always say, "You can tell a Parker when you see one because they all have the same beautiful eyes."

The judge then looked over at Angela and asked, "Are you ok, Ms. Dobson?"

"I'll be fine Your Honor, I'd just like to get this over with," she stated as she turned around and looked at me pitifully.

Chapter 13

Terry

"Man get off of me, you ain't gotta escort me know dayum where. I'm leaving any mothafuckin way," I cursed at the bailiff as I walked to the exit. "That's some foul shit Angela, that's real foul," I stated angrily as I slammed the exit door open and walked out.

I couldn't believe what just happened as I paced the lobby floor. How dare she do this shit to me? How you going to tell someone that you're the father and all along they know damn well you're not. Man, I am so fucking pissed, I just want hit something. I want to hit it hard so that it can feel the pain that I'm feeling now.

"Bae, bae, it's ok, it's ok," Frankie said as he ran up on me and hugged me tightly. "I'm here for you, I'm here for you."

"Why, why would she do that? How could she do that especially taking me through hell all these months when she knew dayum well I wasn't the father, Frankie, how could she?"

"I don't know Terry, I wish I could say something or do something to make you feel better and not hurt but all I can do is be here for you, you know," he said as he continued to hug me.

"Man, I am so fucking piss, you have no idea," I stated as I began to fill the tears well up in my eyes. That's my daughter everyone says so. I don't understand, she looks just like me, Frankie."

"Yeah, she does. Those results just blew me away. The crazy thing is, who is this other man?"

"Look, I can't go back in there but you can. Go in that bitch and find out who it is. Will you do that for me?"

"Ok, but are you going to be ok?"

"I'm fine, I just wanna know," I replied trying to catch my breath and calm down as my heartbeat seemed to be pounding 1000 beats per minute.

James

"Bailiff, can you escort the other gentleman out here from my office please," the judge asked.

I have to be honest, I couldn't wait to see who this man was because Angela has never ever mentioned being with another man. I mean, I know Angela almost as well as she knows herself and for her not to tell me doesn't make any since. We've always have shared our dreams, hopes and secrets.

I noticed as Frankie walked back in the courtroom and he kind of nodded his head over at me I guess to let me know that terry was ok. I nodded my head back in return.

From this point on, everything seemed to have gone in slow motion. I sat there and watched as the bailiff open the door and escorted the other possible father out into the courtroom. I can't even describe the expression on my face other than my jaw dropped to the floor. The distrust at that moment was real. I have been disappointed in my son many times, but this here, is more than I can bare.

"Thank you for coming today Mr. Parker, would you please go over and stand in front of the podium," the judge began. "According to the file, you have the same name as the other potential father, are you guys related?"

"Yes Your Honor, he's my cousin," James Jr. stated.

"Ok, so, you know why you are here?"

"Yes, Your Honor."

I couldn't fathom the image of my own son and Angela being together. My son who is a police officer in Philly has a wife and family. I don't even know how they could have even gotten together. And how could Angela do this to me, she has know James Jr. ever since he was born, hell, she was practically his God-mother.

"Ms. Dobson, is this the last potential father," the judge asked.

"Yes Your Honor," she said with a hint of attitude.

""Ok, well according to DNA Diagnostics, Mr. James Parker Jr. you are the father!"

Again, everything seemed to have been going in slow motion that my son sat down on the bench and appeared to begun crying, Angela stood at the podium like she didn't care one way or the other and Frankie stormed out of the courtroom I guess to tell Terry the news.

I, on the other hand felt numb. I felt betrayed by my son as well as by Angela. And the truth is, this baby girl was not my nephew's child but my son's child which made me this child's grandfather. What am I suppose to feel, now? All that kept running through my mind was, no wonder she looked like a Parker, she was a Parker through and through. She was my son's child, wow.

Once the bailiff called the next case, Angela, James Jr. and myself along with Nicky scrambled to get out into the lobby. I suspected that Angela just wanted to go home. However, I knew it wasn't going to be that easy, not with Terry out there waiting on her. And God only knows what Frankie has already told Terry.

Just as I had thought, Terry, Frankie, James Jr. and Angela stood out in the lobby fussing and cussing one another out. The crazy thing is, I didn't know what to do because I was caught dead in the middle. These people were my family and I loved them all. What could I do? I looked down at Nicky as he grabbed hold of my leg and held it tightly. I knew he must have been scared because he began to cry saying, "Pop-pop, wanna go home."

The next thing I knew was Terry and James Jr. began throwing punches at one another. Here we are, in the courthouse lobby and these fools are fighting. I was so disgusted at them all that I picked Nicky up and carried him out of the courthouse and took him home. I really didn't care what happened at that point to any of them other than the fact that Nicky was safe and that he was with me.

§§§§§

Later that night before going to bed, I walked by Nicky's room and I heard him crying.

"What's wrong Nicky," I asked as I walked in his room and sat on his bed.

"I'm scared Pop-pop."

"What are you scared of?"

"I'm scared you gonna leave me like my father did," he answered wiping his eyes.

My heart almost broke when he said that, I can't imagine not having my parents in my life while growing up as a child. I leaned over and Picky Nicky up and held him in my lap. "You know what, you don't have to be scared son, I'm not going anywhere for a long time."

"You promise."

"I promise, Nicky. It's gonna be just me and you, a'ight?"

After a minute or so, Nicky then asked me, "Do you know if my father is in Heaven?"

"I'm sure he is Nicky. I mean, I think he's been looking down at you this whole time making sure that you are being taken care of. And to make sure, he brought you to me," I answered hugging him tightly.

"Can I sleep in your bed tonight, please," he asked looking up at me with puppy dog eyes.

"Sure, why not. I tell you what, why don't

you get you teddy bear and I'll fix us some hot chocolate and I'll meet you in my room let's say in 5 minutes, cool?"

"Cool."

I then went downstairs to fix us both a cup of hot chocolate and while pulling up some cups in my kitchen cabinet, my cell phone rang and it was Juan. "Hey you," I said answering my phone.

"What in the hell is going on with you people," he asked laughing into the phone.

"What are you talking about?"

"For the last couple of hours I have gotten a call from Angela, Terry, Frankie and your son Junior."

"Oh, so you heard, I gathered," I asked pouring the hot water into the cups.

"I've heard most of it but why haven't you been answering your phone?"

"For what?"

"Because they have been calling me trying to get in touch with you."

"Again, for what?"

"Look, all I know is that while they were in court a fight broke out and they all were arrested and want you to come and bail them out," he snickered.

"Oh really," I laughed.

"Yes, oh really. So what are you going to do James?"

"I'm not going to do anything. They got themselves in that situation. I told them I didn't want to be placed in the middle so let them take care of it the best way they know how," I scoffed.

"Now James, we can't leave them in there. That wouldn't be right," he laughed.

"It wasn't right for them to do what they did. How in the hell you gonna fight someone in the courthouse lobby and not think you going to get locked up, really?"

"Well, I did find out that they did let your son go on his own recognizance. You know because he's a police officer. As for Angela, they let her go as well because they know her, you know? Now, Terry and Frankie are still there waiting to see a JD so they can get a bail amount. I know you're not gonna just let them stay there, are you?"

"Look Juan, I'm about to have a cup of hot chocolate with Nicky and we're going to bed. I will consider everything in the morning. How's that?"

"Ok James, but remember we are only human and we make mistakes. Don't be so hard on family. I wish I wouldn't have been so stubborn and maybe Ken and I would have made up before he died. You know, tomorrow is never promised to anyone. So, keep that in mind and sleep well my friend, smooches."

After hanging up with Juan, I seriously thought about what he had to say and truth is, he is absolutely right. Sometimes we wait too long in telling people we love them or that we're sorry or even say thank you to them.

Once I got upstairs to my room Nicky had already made himself comfortable in my bed watching television. "Well, check you out. I hope you comfortable," I said handing him his hot chocolate.

"Yup," he replied smiling from ear to ear.

"You know Nicky I want you to know how much I love you. You know that right? And I think you are so cool," I said smiling at him.

"I love you to Pop-pop and I think you're cool too," he said putting his hot chocolate down on the nightstand and jumping up on my lap and hugging me.

The Cool In You 2

Mike Warren

51153487R00090

Made in the USA
Charleston, SC
12 January 2016